The Hottest Superstars of Wrestling!

Read all about . . .

Stone Cold Steve Austin
Vince McMahon
Hollywood Hogan
Goldberg
The Undertaker
Kane
The Rock
Scott Steiner
Mankind
"Macho Man" Randy Savage
Ric Flair

. . . and many others! This up-to-date guide tells you all about your favorite wrestlers, from the best of the good guys to villains so bad they make *you* want to leap into the ring! This is *the* source of information about the biggest stars from the weird, wonderful, and wacky world of pro wrestling!

Books by Daniel Cohen

Are You Ready?
Hollywood Dinosaur
The Millennium
Wrestling Renegades

Available from ARCHWAY Paperbacks

Ghostly Tales of Love and Revenge
Ghosts of the Deep
The Ghost of Elvis and Other Celebrity Spirits
The Ghosts of War
Phantom Animals
Phone Call from a Ghost: Strange Tales from Modern America
Real Ghosts

Available from MINSTREL Books

WRESTLING RENEGADES

An In-Depth Look at Today's Superstars of Pro Wrestling

Dan Cohen

AN ARCHWAY PAPERBACK
Published by POCKET BOOKS
New York   London   Toronto   Sydney   Tokyo   Singapore

AN ARCHWAY PAPERBACK *Original*

An Archway Paperback published by
POCKET BOOKS, a division of Simon & Schuster Inc.
1230 Avenue of the Americas, New York, NY 10020

ISBN: 0-671-03674-2

First Archway Paperback printing June 1999

10 9 8 7 6 5 4 3 2 1

AN ARCHWAY PAPERBACK and colophon are registered trademarks of Simon & Schuster Inc.

Front cover photo credits, clockwise from top left: Scott Cunningham/American Sports Gallery, Mitch Layton/Duomo, Scott Cunningham/American Sports Gallery, Scott Cunningham/American Sports Gallery, Gregg DeGuire/London Features, Duomo

Printed in the U.S.A.

IL 4+

To BLAKE A. FARRELL,
World's Greatest Wrestling Fan

CONTENTS

CONTENTS

Introduction—
a Confession

Ok, I admit it. I'm a pro wrestling fan.

In fact, wrestling and I go back a long, long way.

I grew up on the South Side of Chicago. As a teenager in the early 1950s, I would take a streetcar down to the old Marigold Arena to see the Wednesday evening wrestling matches. I didn't go every Wednesday, we didn't have that kind of money. But I went as often as I could.

I saw a lot of the popular wrestlers of the era, like Lou Thesz, who seemed to be the permanent world champion, and Verne Gagne, one of the classiest "scientific" wrestlers of that or any other era. (Chuck Coppock, a Chicago radio personality, described Gagne as "the Eisenhower administration in tights.") There were the Schnabel brothers,

Hans and Fritz, who wrestled both as individuals and as a tag team. They were bad guys—there were a lot of bad-guy wrestlers with German names in the post–World War II era.

In my crowd, the big favorite was Chief Don Eagle. He sported a Mohawk haircut. Years later I learned, much to my surprise, that he really was a Mohawk Indian, though not a chief. His father was Joseph War Hawk, who had wrestled professionally in the 1930s. A few of the braver boys in my high school (I was not among them) actually got Mohawk haircuts in imitation of their hero, an act which horrified our principal. Remember, this was the age of *Ozzie and Harriet.*

My personal favorite was Benito Gardini. He was an unimpressive, tubby little fellow, more of a coward than an actual bad guy. He rarely won a match, in fact, I'm not sure he ever won a match. He spent most of his time in the ring either running away or pleading for mercy. But when an opponent made the mistake of turning his back, Gardini would spring like a tiger and try to claw his eyes out from the rear. Gardini had a great gimmick: Whenever he was thrown to the mat, and that was frequently, he bounced. It was amazing! He looked like a rubber ball! I didn't know how he did it. I still don't.

Much to my regret, I never got a chance to see some of the flashiest wrestlers of the era, like Gorgeous George and Antonino Rocca, in person. But I saw them regularly on television.

In the 1950s, television made wrestling popular with a wide audience. Wrestling, broadcast live, was a cheap way to fill the screen during the early days of TV. But as television became increasingly a part of everyday life and more profitable as well, the networks took control of the programs, and wrestling was replaced by soap operas, westerns, game shows, and variety shows.

The spread of cable television opened up an enormous number of new channels and new opportunities for wrestling on TV. By the mid 1980s, professional wrestling was back on television, bigger and gaudier than ever, and I was back—not only watching it but writing about it.

After a while, interest seemed to fade again until the late 1990s when there was another explosion, and wrestling shows began outdrawing everything else on cable TV and even many network shows, particularly among certain age groups (children, teens, and aging veterans of Marigold Arena).

For nonfans, professional wrestling is like Count Dracula: They keep trying to drive a stake into its heart and kill it once and for all, but it keeps coming back.

What's the appeal?

It's hard to explain to those who don't get it, but let me give you an example. Late in January, I was sort of dozing my way through a lackluster and totally predictable Super Bowl game. The only entertaining thing was a cheeky commercial for the World Wrestling Federation (WWF)—a hilarious sendup of the pretensions of most professional sports.

The WWF also scheduled a championship match during halftime, broadcasting it on a cable network. That match, between Mankind and The Rock, was held in an empty stadium. It started in the ring then continued through the seats, stadium offices, the kitchen (resulting in one of the messiest food fights in television history), and ended on a loading dock where Mankind pinned The Rock with the aid of forklift truck! It was as if the Atlanta Falcons had defeated the Denver Broncos using Cruise missiles.

Even longtime wrestling fans who thought they had seen everything realized they hadn't and were left wondering, "What will they think of next?"

That's the appeal.

CHAPTER 1

From Carnival to Cable

Wrestling is one of the oldest sports in the world—maybe it's *the* oldest. There are pictures of wrestlers in the tombs of the Egyptian pharaohs. The ancient Greeks loved wrestling—it was one of the first sports in the Olympics. The Romans liked it too, though losers could easily wind up dead.

Wrestling was popular in colonial America. George Washington was a champion in the Virginia colony. Abraham Lincoln, who at 6-feet 4-inches tall was a giant in his day, was a skillful wrester. He even wrestled for money, and according to one story he was engaged in a wrestling match when a messenger came to tell him he had been nominated to run for president in 1860.

The roots of today's professional wrestling in America can be found in the carnivals and county fairs of the post–Civil War era. Wrestlers with outlandish costumes, names, and fake biographies would stage exhibition matches or accept challenges from any local strongman. A cash prize was usually offered to anyone who could stay in the ring for fifteen minutes with "the champion." Carneys hated to give up prize money, so if the local guy looked as if he was going to survive, he was maneuvered to a curtain backdrop at one end of the ring. Behind the curtain was another carney with a baseball bat. Professional "champions" rarely lost such challenges.

Another scheme was to make a deal with the local hero and allow him to win. The carney would make money by betting against the "champion." The "champion" usually won the inevitable rematch, and his knowledgeable backers picked up even more money on side bets.

By the end of the nineteenth century, professional wrestling was already well established in Europe. (In Germany, matches were usually staged in beer halls.) As more and more immigrants flooded into American cities, wrestling matches branched out from carnival tents to big city arenas and stadiums.

Professional wrestlers generally cheated when they had to, and many of the matches were fixed. A straight match, however, could be interminable. The winner had to take two out of three falls, and there was no time limit. An 1881 New York match between "Champion" William Muldoon and Clarence Whistler, "The Wonder of the West," lasted over seven hours leaving the spectators sleeping in their seats or demanding their money back. It wasn't until the 1920s that time limits were imposed on wrestling matches.

The first generally recognized American champion was a fellow by the name of Ed Gotch. Gotch was a really good wrestler, but he wasn't much of a sportsman. He hated to lose and would do absolutely anything to win. In one match he covered himself with so much oil that his opponent couldn't get a grip on him. In another he got one of his associates, named Ad Santell, into the training camp of challenger George Hackenschmidt. Before their match, Santell managed to injure Hackenschmidt's knee, though he made it look like an accident. Hackenschmidt wanted to cancel their match, but the promoters had already sold advance tickets and spent the money. He was persuaded to keep the injury secret, but he agreed to wrestle only if Gotch wouldn't embarrass him and let him win one of the three falls. Gotch agreed, but doublecrossed him, and beat the crippled Hackenschmidt in two quick falls. He was not a nice guy.

The next real wrestling superstar was Ed "Strangler" Lewis. His real name was Robert Friedrich, but he took an alias because he didn't want his parents to know what he was doing. Lewis was not only the best wrestler of his day; he was probably the best wrestler there ever was. His signature hold, the head-lock, was so deadly that he couldn't get anyone to train with him and had to practice on a dummy.

The "Strangler" was almost too good. He beat practically everybody so easily that matches became boring. A 1916 bout with Joe Stecher dragged on for five hours and had the fans screaming and throwing their seat cushions into the ring. Finally, Lewis agreed to lose a few matches just to make things interesting. He was well paid for his loss and always won the rematch. In his long career, the "Strangler" had over 6,000 bouts but only 33 losses.

By the time Lewis retired in 1938, America was in the depths of the Great Depression, and wrestling along with most other businesses was in the dumps. Wrestling matches were still being held in small arenas throughout the country, but it didn't really revive until after World War II with the advent of television.

The modern era of wrestling began with a fellow named George Wagner of Seard, Nebraska. Wagner was a fair wrestler, but he was a great showman. His evolution into the phenomenon known as "Gorgeous George" was a slow one. It began with him wearing an elaborately embroidered robe, which he folded slowly and carefully before each match; then he dyed his brown hair blond and had it elaborately waved. As time passed, he began throwing gold-colored bobby pins to the crowd, which booed and jeered but turned out in droves to see him. In addition, his entrance to the ring became more and more elaborate. He was preceded by a valet carrying a little silver tray, and the valet carefully would spray George's corner with perfume. Then George himself would enter to the strains of "Pomp and Circumstance" walking slowly down the aisle while insulting the fans as he went. He would then parade around the ring so everyone could admire him, and sometimes the valet would spray his opponent with perfume. When the referee would try to examine George's hands for grease or other illegal substances, George would shout, "Get your filthy hands off me!" Once the bout started, George behaved pretty much like the typical eye-gouging, biting, rabbit-punching villain of wrestling. But the match itself was almost beside the point. It was the showmanship and personality of the wrestler that brought in the crowds. Everyone knew who Gorgeous George was, even if they had never seen a wrestling match, because television made him a national celebrity.

George kept the act going in and out of the ring. Every time he went to have his hair done it was an event covered by the local media. He was guaranteed $100,000 to bring his act to Madison Square Garden in New York. Radio and television comedians managed to work his name into practically every routine.

You can see how modern professional wrestling really started with Gorgeous George.

Another phenomenon of the early television days was Antonino "Argentine" Rocca.

Rocca had been born in Italy but had emigrated with his parents to Argentina where he began his wrestling career. In America he could appeal to two audiences, Italians and Latinos, but his breathtaking aerial style appealed to everyone. Rocca, who wrestled bare footed, was the master of the flying drop kick and leaps from the top of the ropes. He was really more acrobat than wrestler. Many wrestlers scorned his style, but he became the biggest drawing card of the early 1950s His aerial athleticism changed the face of wrestling.

When wrestling reemerged on cable television in the 1980s, showmanship in and out of the ring predominated. The entrances of today's wrestlers make Gorgeous George's procession to the ring look tame. While Antonino Rocca might leap from the top rope, today's wrestlers leap right out of the ring. An old-time villain might conceal a roll of coins or piece of lead pipe that he would use during a match. Today, folding chairs, tables, and even the ring steps are routinely used to batter opponents.

Long gone are the interminable matches where two men could be locked in a single hold for half an hour. In today's wrestling shows, less than half the time is actually spent wrestling. The rest is taken up with elaborate entrances, cowardly exits, shouting matches, challenges, and the interference of managers, other wrestlers, and the occasional football team or motorcycle gang. An increasing amount of time is now spent covering activities like brawls or ambushes in the locker rooms, the halls, and places outside of the auditorium, such as the parking lot. There are impromptu gang fights, a few kidnappings, and the regular destruction of a limousine or other vehicle.

By the 1980s, professional wrestling had been transformed into a live-action comic book with superbly muscled and costumed superheroes and supervillians. In the 1990s, the lines between hero and villain ("babyface," or "face," and "heel" in wrestling lingo) have blurred a bit, but the showmanship is sharper, gaudier, and more surprising than ever.

Daniel Cohen

CHAPTER 2

The Organizations

Professional wrestling is really controlled by organizations that arrange the matches, hire the wrestlers, give them their names and personalities, and own the TV rights.

Today there are two major organizations or federations in America, the World Wrestling Federation (WWF) and World Championship Wrestling (WCW). Many smaller organizations that arrange local matches and sometimes even have televised shows remain, but the two big ones have all the superstars and completely dominate the professional wrestling world. If you are watching wrestling on television, you are almost certainly watching the WWF or the WCW.

Up until the 1930s, wrestling in America

was handled by a large number of small-time regional promoters, many of whom were former wrestlers or boxing promoters. In 1948 most of the promoters formed a loose organization called the National Wrestling Alliance (NWA), but one notable holdout from the NWA was Capitol Wrestling, run by the McMahon family. Capitol Wrestling had been started by boxing promoter Jess McMahon, who was succeeded by his son Vince McMahon Sr. Although Capitol Wrestling was centered in Washington D.C., it controlled promotions on much of the east coast.

When wrestling became a hit on early television, the McMahon family was able to exploit the new medium most effectively because they already had most of the big-name stars under contract, and because they controlled wrestling in New York, the television center of the world. In 1963 McMahon formed the World Wide Wrestling Federation (WWWF). One of the W's was soon dropped for the sake of brevity.

In 1982 Vince McMahon Jr., the third generation of the wrestling dynasty, took over just in time to take advantage of the new opportunities for wrestling that opened up with the growth of cable television. Vince

McMahon Jr. declared war on the NWA and any other independent wrestling organizations that happened to be around. He tried to buy all of their stars, take over their territory, and drive them out of business. He was ruthless. Later Vince Jr. was to admit, "We did it all with mirrors; it was all cash flow. Had those promoters known that I didn't have any money, they could have killed us." But they didn't know, and Vince Jr. killed them and profited hugely from the explosion of professional wrestling on cable TV during the mid 1980s.

What Vince Jr. understood better than anyone else was that what the public wanted from wrestling was not so much the grunts and the groans but the glitz and the glitter, not the classy scientific moves but the spectacular leaps from the top ropes. To be successful, wrestling had to be entertainment; it had to be showbiz. For examples, there had always been feuds—real and staged—in wrestling but under Vince Jr.'s direction, the feuds expanded into complex, ongoing soap operas. And when Vince Jr. staged his first WrestleMania show on pay TV, he filled the arena and the ring with celebrities like Muhammad Ali, Liberace, Billy Martin, and rock star Cyndi Lauper.

It looked like McMahon and his WWF were going to gain complete control over wrestling; but then a new challenger rode in from Atlanta, cable-TV mogul Ted Turner. Turner realized that wrestling on cable TV was a very good business, but he didn't want it to become a McMahon monopoly, so he bought up the remains of the old NWA and signed on its few top stars, like champion Ric Flair.

According to McMahon, Turner then called him and announced that he was now in the "rasslin" business. "Good," said McMahon, *we're* in the entertainment business," and he then hung up.

Although some of the fights in the ring may be phony, the fight between McMahon and Turner is very real—and it's all about money, lots of money. McMahon had the experience, the contacts, and all the cunning and daring of an old-time carnival showman. Turner had the money. He kept buying up WWF stars, most notably Hulk Hogan in 1994. Hogan had to change his name from "Hulk" to "Hollywood" because the WWF still owned the "Hulk" label. Turner bought up WWF announcers like "Mean" Gene Okerlan and managers like Jimmy "the mouth of the South" Hart. He moved his most popular wrestling show, *Nitro,* from Saturday night to Monday night just to compete directly with the WWF flagship Monday-night show, *Raw.* Ted Turner spent money and lost money for eight years. But he stared down Vince Jr., and he never blinked.

WWF shows still continue to outdraw WCW products, but since all wrestling is more popular than ever before, Turner's investment is now paying off big time, and he has succeeded in his primary goal of preventing McMahon and his WWF from totally dominating televised wrestling.

While the hoopla, the lights, the noise, and even the cast of characters are sometimes almost identical (wrestlers change allegiances between the two organizations regularly) there are some not-so-subtle differences between the two. McMahon, who was born with wrestling promotion in his blood, is ready to do anything, absolutely anything to get an audience. His *Monday Night Raw* show is likely to live up to its name. Turner's presentations are better looking, and while they contain plenty of the good old wrestling vulgarity and mock brutality, they are more like family entertainment—more respectable. McMahon, the old promoter, thinks only in terms of the number of fans in the seats or sitting in front of the TV. Turner, the TV veteran, knows that if you go too far, you are going to lose your advertisers—and the money is in advertising. And if you go *too* far, some of the cable systems might object, and you may turn off potential new fans.

Vince Jr. has always been out front in wrestling. He introduced matches, did interviews, and was a ringside announcer. He has recently recreated himself as the most evil and hated man in wrestling. He has become one of his own organization's biggest draws. The old good-guy, bad-guy wrestling scenario had grown a bit stale. But everybody still hates the boss. So in April 1998, Vince Jr., or *Mr.* McMahon, as everyone now has to call him, began one of the most bitter feuds in wrestling history—not with his real enemy, Ted Turner—but with his own most popular star, "Stone Cold" Steve Austin. He began a campaign to push the tough-talking, working man's hero aside and create a more obedient "corporate" champion. Austin, of course, would have none of it. Wrestlers began lining up on both sides, and Mr. McMahon hatched endless sinister plots to humiliate, dethrone, cripple, kill, or otherwise dispose of his champion. McMahon has even enlisted his son, the fourth generation of McMahon wrestling promoters, into the plot line. Young Shane McMahon has come off as wonderfully arrogant, devious, and generally as a chip off the old block. The fans have loved it. *Monday Night Raw* ratings have gone through the roof, and WWF pay-per-view shows are attracting more viewers than much more highly publicized boxing matches.

In contrast, Ted Turner is not about to step into a steel cage with Goldberg. In fact, Turner doesn't ever appear at matches, but the WCW also has its own complex employee-relations problems. The president of the WCW is sometime wrestler Eric Bischoff, and he is currently aligned with Hollywood Hogan's rebel or "outlaw" group, the New World Order or nWo. He is now opposed by the WCW, which is being led by many-times-champion "Nature Boy" Ric Flair. Both Bischoff, who is not much of a wrestler, and Flair, who is way past his prime, will get into the ring with one another. Early in 1999 Bischoff was knocked senseless by Flair's nineteen-year-old son, who had concealed a roll of quarters in his hand for a match. Flair replaced Bischoff as president of the organization, but when last seen, Bischoff was still hatching plots to get back on top.

So there it is, the two major wresting organizations are apparently at war with themselves but are really at war with one another. In wrestling, things are rarely what they seem. In fact, they are never what they seem.

CHAPTER 3

Is It Real?

It is not a smart idea to accuse a professional wrestler of being a fake.

A few years back, John Stossel, consumer reporter for ABC's 20/20, did just that to wrestler Dr. D (David Schultz). The good doctor clapped him over the ears so hard that Stossel believed that his hearing had been permanently damaged.

Comedian Richard Belzer challenged Hulk Hogan to put a headlock on him. Hogan did just that, with such force that it cut off the blood supply to the comedian's brain. When Hogan released the hold, Belzer dropped to the floor unconscious.

Goldberg doesn't appreciate being called a fake. He has challenged anyone to stand up to his trademark move, the spear ram, in which the 285-pound mountain of muscle charges headfirst from about 10 feet away. If anyone can stand up after the charge, "they can call it a fake," says Goldberg—but not before. Wisely, there have been no takers for that challenge.

Back in the 1950s there was serious discussion about whether wrestling was "real" or not. Fans, particularly young fans like myself, thought it was "real-real." Certainly most of us had our moments of doubt, but that didn't arise while we were watching a match, and doubts didn't interfere with our enjoyment. Those who didn't appreciate wrestling generally dismissed it as a complete fake.

Wrestlers themselves don't like to seriously discuss the reality of wrestling. You're likely to get an answer like the one Hulk Hogan gave, "For those who believe, you don't need an explanation; for those who don't believe, no amount of explaining will do."

But wrestling isn't just a matter of faith. Something is really going on in that ring. Looked at coldly, it should be clear that if everything that appeared to be happening in a match actually *was* happening, the police would be called because someone would be seriously injured or killed.

When a 280-pound man jumps from the top ring rope onto his opponent, who is lying flat on the canvas, the result is going to be, at the very least, a lot of broken ribs. Unless, of course, the jumper makes a very serious and successful attempt not to injure his opponent by not quite landing on him or by landing in a way in which knees, elbows, or other bony parts don't make the impact. The result of the jump can still be painful but not deadly or dangerous.

If a wrestler is repeatedly punched or kicked viciously, he is not going to be able to get up from the canvas and do the same to his opponent a minute later, unless the punches and kicks are "pulled" so that they have very little power in them.

Nobody is going to get up after being hit viciously in the back of the head with a steel folding chair, unless he hasn't really been hit in the head but across the back instead, and the chair has not been swung as viciously as it appears. The blow is going to sting, but it's not going to be lethal.

Moves like the clothesline and forearm

smash are popular because they can be made to look spectacular, but they don't do any real damage.

A toehold applied by a strong and skillful wrestler can easily break a man's leg. But if that skillful wrestler does not apply full pressure, the hold is going to look a lot worse than it is.

And how about a wrestler picking up and then body slamming someone who weighs a lot more than he does? The big fellow has to give the little guy a bit of help by jumping into his arms and grabbing his trunks to steady the hold. If the big guy was really struggling to get away, the little guy couldn't handle him. But in the match it doesn't look like the big guy is cooperating.

What goes on in the ring is no action-adventure film. The leaps and falls are not accomplished by trick photography. The wrestler can't call in a stunt man to take the blows for him. There is both pain and danger in every match. Sometimes injuries are faked in order to give a wrestler time off or build up anticipation about the rematch. But there are plenty of real injuries as well, and there have been a few deaths in the ring. A really good wrestler is the one who can make the blows and the holds look more devastating than they really are but not put his opponent out of business.

It takes years of training, talent, and a lot of courage to make it big in professional wrestling. If you see some of the more inexperienced or less talented wrestlers on the minor circuits, their matches really do look fake. In the big time, however, it's very hard to tell what is real and what isn't.

That's why professional wrestlers tend to bristle when they are told wrestling is "fake." It may not be real-real, but for the fan it's a great show, and it's quite real enough. These individuals are real athletes and real professionals.

In the late 1980s Vince McMahon finally settled the reality question in wrestling when he began describing WWF wrestling as "sports entertainment" rather than pure sports. It wasn't that McMahon had a sudden attack of truthfulness. What he wanted was to get his business out from under the control of state and local athletic commissions. For their part, most athletic commissions were quite happy to relinquish control over professional wrestling. It had always been something of an embarrassment, and they never quite knew what to do with it.

There was some fear that McMahon's admission would alienate fans. In fact, it seems to have had the opposite effect because the popularity of wrestling has jumped both on television and in the arenas. A lot of people seem genuinely relived to know that the guys in the ring aren't going to get killed or maimed. That allows them to relax and enjoy the show.

Still, wrestlers don't like to spend a lot of time talking about the tricks of their trade. It's important to maintain the illusion and to allow the fans, you and me, to engage in what writers of fiction call "the willing suspension of disbelief."

Watching wrestling is a lot like watching stage magic. You know it isn't real, that the lady really isn't being sawed in half. But it looks so darn real that you can't figure out exactly how it's done, and you marvel at the skill of the performer.

CHAPTER 4

Referees and Rules

The most thankless job in the world is referee in a professional wrestling match.

There they are in those silly looking striped shirts and bow ties, running around the ring, and nobody is paying the slightest attention to them. They are regularly intimidated by shouting from violent men three or four times their size. They are distracted by crafty or crazed managers, half-naked women, and the appearance of crowds of wrestlers or others who are not supposed to be in the match. Occasionally referees are knocked cold. Sometimes that's part of the story line, but sometimes it just happens by accident.

Usually referees who are small, unknown, and poorly paid are not hurt and play only a minor part in the ring drama. It's different for celebrity referees. When the referee is someone like Mike Tyson, you can figure he is going to have an impact on the outcome. And when Vince McMahon Jr. referees a "Stone Cold" Steve Austin match, it is safe to assume he is not neutral and will probably be knocked to the canvas—repeatedly.

The biggest "problem" an ordinary referee has is to look as if he is enforcing the rules. Does professional wrestling really have rules? Yes, it does—sort of—some of the time.

There are rules about how a match is won. The most common way is the "pin fall." One contestant pins an opponent's shoulders to the mat for a three count. Sometimes the referee counts slowly, 1 . . . 2 . . . 3; other times it's a quick 123. Usually it's just 1, 2 because the one who is about to be pinned must be able to kick out, twist out, or get a foot on the ropes. Sometimes someone else charges in from outside the ring and clobbers the individual on top.

A "count out" is another way to win a match. The rules say that a wrestler who is out of the ring for twenty seconds can be counted out, and his opponent will win.

Today, about half the action in a match takes place outside of the ring. Have you ever seen anyone lose a match by a count out? Probably not. The rules also state that the other wrestler, like a boxer, must go to a neutral corner before the count starts. In fact, what usually occurs is that one wrestler throws his opponent out of the ring and then jumps out after him. Most wrestlers just ignore the count-out rule because it would be an unexciting and disappointing end to a match.

There are also rules about disqualification. If a wrestler brings a foreign object, like a chair, a stun gun, or a bunch of his friends, into the ring to help him he can be disqualified. Sometimes that happens. And sometimes it doesn't.

A common way of ending a match is by a submission hold, a hold that is so painful and dangerous that a wrestler is forced to give up. Many wrestlers have their favorite submission holds: Ric Flair used to rely on his figure-four leglock, and Lex Luger has his horizontal backbreaker. Once these holds are applied, it is usally all over for an opponent. There are other holds like the sleeper which puts pressure on the neck and, when properly applied, can cause an opponent to simply pass out. Of course, an unconscious man can't say "I give up," so it's up to the referee to determine if a wrestler is able to continue.

The referee is supposed to be able to break an illegal hold at the count of 10, and if the hold isn't broken the offender is disqualified. Let's say one of the competitors has an illegal choke hold on the other and is trying to squeeze the life out of him. The "ref" taps him on the shoulder, tells him to break the hold, and starts counting to 10. Fair enough—but there is loophole in this rule big enough to drive a hearse through. The choker lets go for about a nanosecond, then he clamps the illegal hold on again, and the count starts over. Disqualifications for illegal holds are rare and may be virtually extinct today.

Different types of special matches require different rules, or no rules at all. The increasingly popular "hardcore" matches in the WWF don't even make a pretense of having rules. Their big attraction is that there are no rules, and a wrestler can be pinned anywhere in the arena, and perhaps anywhere in the world, and it still counts. Admittedly the differences between a hardcore match and a standard match are often a little difficult to determine, but hardcore wrestlers usually look meaner and uglier than the other guys.

The rules for a tag-team match state that only one member of each team is "legally" in the ring at a time. The other team member stands on the ring apron clutching in one hand a short piece of rope that is attached to the ring post. The only way a wrestler is supposed to be able to get his partner into the ring is to reach over and touch or tag his hand. It is always harder for a referee to keep track of four wrestlers rather than just two, so tag-team rules tend to be broken more frequently than others. Today, with the addition of interfering managers, bodyguards, girlfriends, and hired assassins at ringside, you can pretty well forget about tag-team rules. Add to that an increasing tendency for tag-team partners to double-cross one another during a match and refuse to go in the ring when tagged, or actually to join the other side. As they say on that other wildly popular TV event *The X-Files*, "Trust no one."

Many matches have special rules or "stipulations." For example, in most championship matches the belt can not change hands as the result of a disqualification, thus giving the champion a huge advantage. He can do just about anything, and the worst that will happen to him is that he will be disqualified, but he will still be champ.

In battle-royal matches, many wrestlers crowd into the ring, usually at three-minute intervals. All the wrestlers battle each other, and the last man left standing in the ring is declared the winner. A combatant is out of the match when he is thrown from the ring over the top rope.

The legendary Andre the Giant, "the Eighth Wonder of the World," was the ultimate master of the battle royal. Towering 7-feet 5-inches tall and weighing over 500 pounds, he was absolutely the biggest man in wrestling and during the 1980s was one of the most popular. He would just stand in the middle of the ring and throw his opponents out. It was always assumed that no one in wrestling could pick him up. Then on March 28, 1987, the wrestling world was stunned when Hulk Hogan bodyslammed Andre in a championship match. It is widely suspected that the Giant, whose career was winding down at the time, gave Hogan a bit of help. But that historic maneuver did not happen during a battle royal, where Andre the Giant remained the undisputed king of the ring.

A recent innovation is the ladder match. Something of value, such as a championship belt or, as in a recent WCW match, a stun gun, is hung high above the ring. The only way to reach it is to climb a ladder placed in the middle of the ring. As a result, two or more huge men attempt to climb up a ladder and try to keep their opponents off the ladder. There are very few effective rules in this event.

One of the most enduring novelty matches (a strangely benign name for this sort of a fight) is the steel-cage match. Basically, a 15-foot-high cage of chain-link steel is constructed around the ring, and the two (or more) wrestlers are locked inside to fight to the finish. There are no rules in such a match, at least no rules that make any difference. Steel-cage matches have been part of wrestling for a long time, but they seem so brutal because wrestlers really can get hurt by being slammed up against the steel mesh. There is a lot of blood spilled in steel-cage matches, particularly if some of the steel mesh is barbed wire. As a result, steel-cage matches are rarely shown on television, yet they remain popular with the fans. The words "in a steel cage" act like a magnet for the true wrestling fanatic. A steel-cage match seems like the ultimate challenge. Recently, these matches have been cleaned up a bit—now there is little or no blood—and the steel-cage match has become a regular part of televised wrestling.

CHAPTER 5

Governor Ventura!
President Hogan?

The biggest wrestling news of 1998 wasn't made in the ring. It was made in the voting booth.

The voters of Minnesota upset all predictions and elected onetime wrestler Jesse "the Body" Ventura governor. It was a huge, and hugely unexpected, victory. He beat Democratic candidate Hubert H. Humphrey 3d, son of the former vice president, and Republican Mayor Norm Coleman of St. Paul.

Ventura was the candidate of the Reform Party, which had been founded by Ross Perot but had never won a statewide office anywhere, ever. Ventura didn't use Perot's millions to gain the victory either. He was outspent more than five to one by the other candidates.

Athletes have been elected to public office before, but none of them were quite like Ventura. Back in the 1980s when Ventura was still active in the ring, *Wrestling All Stars* magazine described him this way: "Ventura is a freak of sorts, with multicolored hair that is red, yellow, blue, orange, and green. He wears at least a half-dozen earrings into the ring and often a custom-tailored T-shirt from a popular New York sex club."

And then there were the sun glasses. He had a collection of sun glasses that would make those once worn by Elton John look conservative. And you can't overlook the jewel that he wore in the cleft of his chin.

"He wasn't really a very good wrestler, but he had charisma," said Dave Meltzer, publisher and editor of the *Wrestling Observer* newsletter. "His best move was standing on the apron yelling at the fans while his tag team partner did all the work."

Because Ventura seemed to be a better talker than wrestler, he pretty much abandoned the ring to become a ringside announcer and commentator for the WWF. He spent most of his time badmouthing all the

good guys and promoting the bad guys—
particularly Jesse Ventura. To Ventura, everyone else was "Jack," and he began referring to himself as "the Body." He was such a
good and persistent talker that folks began
referring to him as Jesse "the Mouth" Ventura.

Ventura left wrestling in 1986 and got
some small roles in films like *Batman and
Robin* and *Predator* with Arnold Schwarzen-
egger. He also became host of a talk-radio
show, and his loud, gravelly, and aggressive
voice became familiar to the people of his
native Minnesota.

"The Body" was born James George Janos,
still his legal name. He started to call himself
Jesse Ventura at the start of his professional
wrestling career in 1975. He saw the name
Ventura on a California map, and it sounded
like it fit the bleached-blond surfer-wrestler
image he was cultivating at the time. Before
becoming a wrestler, he had a stint with the
Navy in Vietnam. Under Minnesota law, a
candidate may run under the name he com-
monly uses—and James George Janos ran
under the more well-known name of Jesse
Ventura.

At first his candidacy was regarded as a
joke, but Ventura did well in debates. He was

relaxed, funny, and sounded like an ordinary, straight-talking guy; a marked contrast to his rather stiff and formal opponents who looked and sounded like professional politicians—which is what they were. Ventura could claim a little political experience, as he had been part-time mayor of the suburb where he lived.

Ventura didn't have a lot of money for slick TV ads, but he used what he did have well and produced one of the best political ads of that or any other election. It showed an apparently nude and heavily bronzed Ventura sitting in the pose of the famous statue *The Thinker*. As the camera panned in for a close-up, the "statue" winked. Ventura began calling himself Jesse "the Mind." He had abandoned his sunglasses, earrings, jeweled chin, and multicolored hair. In fact, he abandoned hair altogether and shaved his head—but he was still recognizably and proudly Jesse Ventura, former pro wrestler.

As he began moving up in the pre-election polls, his opponents still didn't take him seriously, the media didn't take him seriously, and one gets the impression that Ventura didn't really take himself too seriously. Even the people who voted for him may not have taken him seriously. They liked him, but they didn't think he had a chance of winning. But he did.

Immediately, Ventura became the biggest political story in the country—and a huge celebrity. Even this brash loudmouth sounded humbled and awestruck—for a moment anyway. How he will do as governor facing a legislature where the Senate is controlled by the Democrats and the House by the Republicans is something that only time will tell. During the campaign a reporter asked Ventura how he would deal with the legislature. Silently, he slowly raised one of his bulging biceps. It was a memorable moment in American politics.

Governor Ventura action figures showing Jesse in a business suit and his old Navy SEAL uniform (but not his wrestling tights and multicolored hair) are projected to be big sellers during the 1999 Christmas season. "I'm sure going to get one," said one popular wrestler. "It may be my only chance to squeeze Jesse."

No professional wrestler worth his tights was going to ignore the kind of publicity opportunity that Ventura's win created. Hollywood (Hulk) Hogan said that he would love to get Ventura in the ring "one more time before he becomes President." Later,

Hogan decided that since he had beaten Ventura every time they met, he, Hogan, was the better man, and that he deserved to become President.

So on Thanksgiving Night, 1998, Hogan went on *The Tonight Show* and announced that he was retiring from professional wrestling in order to run for President. Hogan wouldn't be the first wrestler to run for President, since Gorgeous George did it in 1952. The Gorgeous One's campaign manager was another wrestler, Chief Jay Strongbow (born Joe Scarpa).

Hogan told host Jay Leno that after Ventura won, a lot of people began calling Hogan and said that he should run for something because he was bigger and more popular than Ventura ever had been. Whereupon he began saying, "Yeah, maybe I'll be the next President of the United States, but I won't take a pay cut! Then the media jumped on it, as the phone calls kept coming in, I said, 'Wow,' you know, 'If I really get serious about this thing, I probably could win.'"

Hogan made one promise that no other candidate could make. He said that he would wrestle Saddam Hussein in a steel-cage match.

Consumer advocate Ralph Nader, who has

also run for President, didn't think Hogan could actually win, but he did take the candidacy seriously. He figured that Hogan could get as much as 10 percent of the vote. "That turnout could affect the dynamics of the other major candidates. It could tip certain federal and state races, fuel satire, and make mockery a frequent voter reaction."

Almost immediately after promising that he was retiring from wrestling in order to run for President, Hogan began acting like a real politician: He broke his promise and got back in the ring. He won the WCW championship in a match that looked phony even by pro wrestling standards. He once again took active charge of the nWo and had it operating in its usual dastardly way.

Was Hogan back in wrestling, or was he just getting warmed up for a career in Washington? Who knows? This is wrestling, where anything, quite literally anything at all, can and does happen.

CHAPTER 6

Hollywood (Hulk) Hogan

He is the most recognizable wrestler in the world today and has been for over a decade. More than any other individual, he brought professional wrestling into the mainstream and vastly expanded its audience.

Hollywood (Hulk) Hogan didn't begin life wanting to be a wrestler. He didn't even begin named Hogan. He was born Terry Bolla, on August 11, 1953 in Venice Beach, California, and he wanted to be a rock musician. In fact, wrestling promoters first spotted him playing bass guitar in a nightclub in the 1970s. The promoters weren't impressed by his musical abilities, but they were impressed by his size (6 feet 7 inches, 275 pounds) and by his charisma.

The promoters gave him his name too. He was first Terry "the Hulk" Boulder. The "Hulk" part came from the popular Marvel comics character or, more specifically, from bodybuilder Lou Ferrigno, who played the green-skinned character in a TV series.

The promoters also gave him the Hogan name. "When I first started wrestling," he explained, "the wrestling world was very territorial. They had Italian wrestlers, and they had Native Americans, and they had wrestlers for the Polish people. They said, 'You should be Hogan.' 'Yeah,' they said, 'You should be Hulk Hogan. Put some red dye in your hair, and you'll be an Irishman.'"

Despite his catchy new name and always impressive physique, Hogan's career didn't take off at first. In 1979 he was wrestling in the WWF and was managed by the evil Freddie Blassie. Hogan was one of Blassie's stable of bad guys. But he could never defeat the reigning champion, Bob Backlund. He then spent several years in the smaller (and now defunct) American Wrestling Association (AWA) before returning to the WWF. Hulk Hogan's real career breakthrough came when he appeared with Sylvester Stallone in *Rocky III*, in which he played a loudmouthed wrestler named Thunder Lips.

In 1984 Hulk Hogan reached the top of his profession when he defeated the hated Iron Sheik and became WWF heavyweight champion. Hulk Hogan, who had started as a bad guy, became the ultimate good guy, the symbol of America, and an ideal hero to the kids. That marked the beginning of the phenomena known as "Hulkamania." Hogan was the undisputed star of the early pay-per-view WrestleManias, the most successful wrestling shows ever.

Hogan's most famous match came at WrestleMania III when he bodyslammed and then pinned the hitherto unbeatable and legendary Andre the Giant, "the Eighth Wonder of the World." If Andre wasn't the biggest wrestler in history, he was darn near the biggest at a height of 7 feet 4 inches and weighing nearly 500 pounds. Yet Hogan was able to bodyslam the Giant and pin him, and a new legend was born.

Hogan parlayed his growing popularity into an industry of Hulk Hogan toys, tee shirts, cartoons, and more movie and TV appearances. In 1994 he became the only professional wrestler to appear on the cover of *Sports Illustrated* magazine.

He won and lost the WWF title five times, defeating such opponents as "Macho Man"

Randy Savage, Sergeant Slaughter, and the Undertaker. He lost his WWF title for the last time to his most persistent and mysterious opponent, The Ultimate Warrior. Then in 1993 he retired to pursue a career in movies and television, but the work bored him. He told *TV Guide*, "I was sitting in those trailers for twelve hours a day going, 'What am I doing here? I could still wrestle. I'm not that old.'"

About that time, representatives from Ted Turner's well-financed WCW came around with a lucrative contract, so Hogan decided to go back into the ring, but for his old employer's arch rival. He couldn't take the nickname "Hulk" with him—that was still owned by the WWF—so he was rechristened "Hollywood" Hogan, partly because of his film career and his wealthy Hollywood lifestyle, though he actually lives in Florida with his wife and two children when he is not on the road.

Though he had a new name, Hogan's persona in the WCW was that of the same blond good guy he had been for years in the WWF. In his very first match he took the WCW title from perennial WCW champ Ric Flair, but somehow the fans didn't respond to Hogan as they had in the past. Perhaps it was the switch of organizations, perhaps it was a change in what wrestling fans liked—but for the first time in a very long time, Hogan was getting booed.

Then WCW president Eric Bischoff suggested to Hogan that he reinvigorate his career by doing what so many other wrestlers had done in the past—switch personalities. So Hulk Hogan, the shining example of wrestling virtue, truly became Hollywood Hogan, an egotistical, loud-mouthed, cowardly character who would do anything, absolutely anything to win.

Hogan became the leader of the New World Order (nWo), a rebel or outlaw clan within the WCW that also listed other big bad guys among its members such as Kevin Nash, Scott Hall, and Scott Steiner.

The new, evil Hogan dressed almost exclusively in black and white, the colors of the nWo. He now sported a stubbly black beard highlighted by a blond, nearly white Fu Manchu moustache. While the fans may not have warmed to the old Hulk Hogan anymore, the new Hollywood Hogan became the man they loved to hate. Hogan and his nWo helped to boost the popularity of the WCW to new heights.

There have been complaints that Hogan is

too old to really wrestle effectively anymore. He has been mercilessly ridiculed on WWF broadcasts. Today, he loses as many matches as he wins, and he no longer appears as often as he used to. When he does appear, there is often a lot more talking than wrestling.

Hogan is certainly no longer the overpoweringly dominant figure that he had been in the mid 1980s. But he is still the most famous and recognizable wrestler in the world, and the man who more than anyone else symbolizes modern professional wrestling.

Hollywood (Hulk) Hogan's place in wrestling history is secure.

CHAPTER 7

"Stone Cold" Steve Austin

"Stone Cold" Steve Austin is arguably the most popular wrestler in America today. Few of the more recent fans of the bullet-headed, tough-talking working man's hero realize that he started his wrestling life as a blond.

Actually, he started life as Steven Williams, a self-confessed redneck, born in Victoria, Texas in 1965. He really was the sort of blue-collar guy that now forms the basis of his wrestling image. Before becoming a wrestler, he had loaded trucks. Austin began wrestling in 1989 with the old NWA, but when that organization disappeared he moved over to the new WCW. He first gained a measure of fame as "Stunning Steve," as part of the Hollywood Blonds tag team with his partner "Flyin'" Brian Pillman. Both men sported shoulder-length blond hair, and they were very successful, holding the WCW tag-team championship for much of 1993.

But then things began to go sour with WCW management. The team was broken up, and Austin wasn't getting the caliber of matches he wanted wrestling solo. In 1995 he was fired by the WCW. The reasons given for the firing depend on whom you ask.

According to Austin, he was dumped after he injured WCW president Eric Bischoff. According to Bischoff, the problem was that Austin himself was getting injured too often, and he was difficult to communicate with.

Whatever the reason, Austin was bitter after the split. In a few months, he was back wrestling for ECW (originally Eastern Championship Wrestling, later Extreme Championship Wrestling). ECW is a small organization that is popular with the more hardcore fans who favor violence over pure showmanship. He wasn't "Stunning Steve" anymore. He emerged as wrestling's angriest man, with a shaved head and the title "Stone Cold."

Austin says he got his new persona after watching a TV special on serial killers. He claims it gave him the concept of a guy who basically doesn't care about anyone. Austin is just a bit embarrassed about the success of his new character. "I don't endorse serial killers in any way, shape, or form," he insists.

Austin's growing popularity was noticed by the WWF, and in 1996 he signed up with Vince McMahon's organization. He had not yet fully perfected the Stone Cold character, so he started in the WWF as The Ringmaster, who was managed by Ted DiBiase, "The Million Dollar Man." But soon he emerged as "Stone Cold," wrestling's icon of rage, and a man who couldn't be managed by anybody.

He became the ultimate blue-collar wrestler—the idol of every working stiff who wanted to tell his boss where to go and how to get there. Austin often arrives at an arena in a pickup truck or on a motorcycle. While other wrestlers favor limousines, Steve Austin's limo was mounted on a monster-truck body, and he drove it over the cars of several of his enemies in an arena parking lot.

Stone Cold struck a chord with WWF fans and quickly rose to the top of the heap. His popularity rivaled Hulk Hogan's in his glory days. In fact, Stone Cold Steve Austin T-shirts and other items have outsold Hogan's at his peak.

Austin, at 6 feet 2 inches and 252 well-muscled pounds, is an impressive and intimidating figure. He would not go unnoticed if you were standing next to him on the bus. But in the world of professional wrestling, where the participants tend to giantism, he is not particularly large or impressively muscled. Actually, among wrestlers he's a pretty ordinary looking guy.

And in a world of outsized muscles and egos, he can sound almost modest. Austin told an interviewer for *TV Guide* that he had taken more than 200 stitches in his face. "There's people with more," he admitted. "I"m just giving you my statistics."

What sets Stone Cold apart from most other wrestlers and makes him the unquestioned superstar that he is today is his attitude, and the way he is able to project it. When he storms into the ring, glares out at the crowd with an icy stare, and shouts, "Hell, yeah!" in a voice that's nine parts fury and one part sandpaper, he can set 20,000 fans in a packed arena into a frenzy of wild cheering that is echoed by millions of fans at home glued to their TV sets. And when

Austin chases his boss, Vince McMahon, through the corridors of an arena and then slams him to the concrete floor with a steel folding chair, the cheers get even louder if possible.

One of McMahon's most brilliant concepts is the development of a "story line"—words he uses freely to describe the elaborate twists and turns of wrestling's ongoing soap opera—where he has become not only Austin's boss, but his chief nemesis. Mr McMahon and his "corporation," a collection of unusually thuggish wrestlers, are out to destroy the career, and ultimately the existence, of the angry loner Stone Cold. Just why a wrestling promoter would want to get rid of his star performer and main meal ticket is not made entirely clear, but this is wrestling—it doesn't have to make sense, it just has to be popular.

This scenario has made Austin not quite a hero, or to use the old wrestling term, "babyface" or good guy. No traditional wrestling babyface would try to beat his opponent to a pulp with a steel folding chair. But compared to McMahon, everybody's lousy boss and the ultimate villain, the angry loner Austin is someone fans can admire and identify with.

Recently Stone Cold has been frequently

identified as "The Rattlesnake." Whether this new name indicates the emergence of a new Austin persona is impossible to say yet.

Like most successful professional wrestlers, Steve Austin loves his work. He makes a great deal of money and standing in front of 20,000 or 50,000 screaming fans "is a pure adrenaline rush." He says that if he ever gets tired of wrestling or is forced out by age or injury, he would like to try some Hollywood acting. He has already appeared as a character in at least one network drama. Other wrestlers, notably Hulk Hogan, have successfully made the crossover.

Stone Cold hasn't talked about running for President—yet.

CHAPTER 8
Goldberg

Usually professional wrestlers have to spend years "in the minors," that is, wrestling for some of the smaller organizations, in small arenas and auditoriums, and on the undercard of major events. Sometimes they serve an apprenticeship getting "squashed," that is, being beaten thoroughly and quickly by big-name wrestlers. That didn't happen to Bill Goldberg. He was an overnight wrestling success.

Goldberg made his professional wrestling debut with the WCW in September 1997, and after an incredible string of matches in which he was not only undefeated but tremendously exciting, Goldberg beat Hollywood Hogan for the WCW championship in

"Stone Cold" Steve Austin
(Pacha/Corbis)

Diamond Dallas Page with the advantage.
(Todd Kaplan/ Star File)

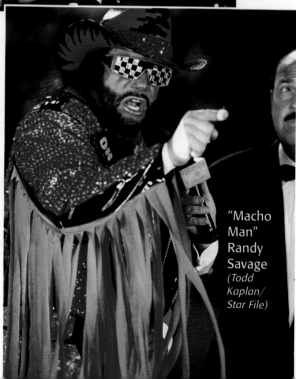

"Macho Man" Randy Savage
(Todd Kaplan/ Star File)

The Undertaker
(Photofest)

Scott Hall corners Ric Flair.
(Todd Kaplan/ Star File)

Sting puts Hollywood Hogan in pain.
(Todd Kaplan/ Star File)

Hollywood Hogan
(Todd Kaplan/Star File)

Goldberg
*(Markus Cuff/
Corbis)*

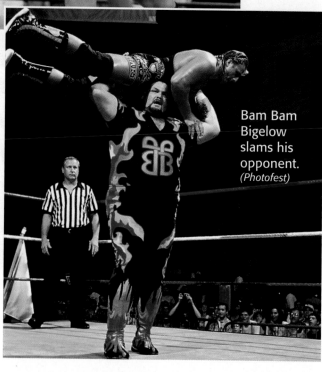

**Bam Bam
Bigelow
slams his
opponent.**
(Photofest)

Kevin Nash
(Todd Kaplan/ Star File)

Nash ignores the ref's warning.
(Todd Kaplan/Star File)

The New World Order: Lex Luger, Scott Steiner,
Hollywood Hogan, Kevin Nash, Buff Bagwell, Scott Hall
(Todd Kaplan/Star File)

July 1998. No wrestler has ever moved from novice to champion that quickly. His "jackhammer" and particularly "the spear" became the most lethal and most feared moves in WCW wrestling. Goldberg continued his unbeaten streak with a series of quick wins (most of his matches lasted just a minute or so) until he was beaten by Scott Hall in December 1998. Of course, Hall had a lot of help from his nWo friends, and Goldberg pulverized him in a rematch a month later.

Bill Goldberg hadn't planned to be a wrestler, but he was big, strong and muscular, and had always been an athlete. The middle son of a Harvard-educated doctor and a classically trained musician, Goldberg grew up with two brothers in Tulsa, Oklahoma. He became a football star at the University of Georgia. He went on to the NFL, where he was a defensive lineman for the Atlanta Falcons. Then a serious injury threatened his professional football career and made him start thinking about another line of work.

Goldberg had never considered a professional wrestling career, but he had always been a weight lifter and body builder, so he knew a lot of professional wrestlers. It was Diamond Dallas Page who persuaded him to give wrestling a try. He did, with spectacular results.

Goldberg has one of the less bizarre personas in wrestling today. He growls a bit and sticks his tongue out a lot, but in wrestling that's understatement. He freely admits, "we're high-paid choreographers" but adds, "we don't do anything fake. The only thing we do is act a bit, but the work is dangerous."

Like every other wrestler, he insists that wrestling is a serious athletic pursuit. And no one but a superbly trained and conditioned athlete could do the sort of things in a ring that the professionals do without being badly injured or killed.

"My ring persona," he says, "does not depend on gimmicks. Basically, what you see is what you get." He even uses his own name.

What you see is a magnificently muscled, 6-foot 4-inch, 285-pound behemoth who scorns the fancy costumes favored by so many of his fellow wrestlers. He favors black trunks, black boots, a shaved skull, and a stare of such intense fury that opponents are often intimidated. His appearance in the auditorium amid a blaze of lights, a shower of sparks, and chants of "gold-BERG, gold-BERG" from frenzied fans is always a thrilling moment.

Goldberg's greatest asset as a wrestler, aside from his enormous strength, is his intensity. Goldberg spends an hour or more before each match pacing up and down, getting psyched up for what is to come. But his opponents have noticed this and have tried, with increasing success to distract him and throw him off his game. They have goaded him into impromptu fights outside the ring, in auditorium parking lots, for example.

For a wrestler, Goldberg isn't a big talker or bragger. His interviews are often as short as his matches. He doesn't habitually threaten to rip an opponent's face off or steal his girl friend. His usual threat is a simple, but sincere, "You're next!" Goldberg has not yet become involved in the Byzantine world of WCW wrestling politics. He has no manager and no gang or outlaw group to rush into the ring to help him out, though a bunch of his old Atlanta Falcon teammates did show up and make their presence felt at one match.

Goldberg relishes his fame. When he was a football player, few people recognized him or asked for his autograph. But when he had a chance to visit Mark McGwire in the St. Louis Cardinals' locker room during the slugger's record-breaking 1998 season, the slugger asked Goldberg for his autograph for his son, who was a wrestling fan and had turned his father into one.

Goldberg also admits that his parents were horrified at first when they found out he was going to be a professional wrestler. "But now that I am one of the most successful Jewish athletes since the beginning of time, they've caught on like wildfire."

Sports broadcaster Bill "Stagger" Lee Marshell wrote that "Goldberg is not only winning matches and the hearts of fans worldwide, but it seems there's an undercurrent of ethnic pride being experienced. . . . It seems that Goldberg has captured the attention and created a new sense of ethnic pride among Jewish fans."

Another sports broadcaster said that he mentioned Goldberg at a very staid fundraiser for the United Jewish Appeal, "and the crowd went nuts. There is something here that does not compute."

But maybe it does compute. Goldberg has said, "We've been able to transform everybody into a kid—at least at heart. We have been able to reach the masses because professional wrestling is, bottom line, fun."

CHAPTER 9

The Undertaker

"The Undertaker" has a real name. It's Mark Calloway, and he was born on March 24, 1962, in Dallas, Texas. He's married, and when not on the road, he lives with his wife, Jodi Lynne, and his two sons in Nashville, Tennessee.

But he won't acknowledge any of that. He will not respond to the name "Mark," but when he is feeling friendly, which is practically never, he will respond to the nickname "The Taker."

All this personal information is known because Mark Calloway had been around wrestling a long time before the apperance of the Undertaker. Back in the late 1980s, when Mark Calloway began wrestling for the old

NWA, it was under the name "Mean Mark Callous." When asked about that, the Undertaker will say only, "Mean Mark Callous is dead." You are not encouraged to ask any more questions along that line. He has wrestled under a number of different names, including Texas Red, but by the time he joined the WWF, he had grown his hair long, put on dark clothes, and adopted the name of The Undertaker—he was also sometimes called The Dead Guy, but that never stuck.

The Undertaker is one of the most closely held and successful personas in professional wrestling today. He is now said to come from "the Beyond" or "Parts Unknown," not Dallas.

When the Undertaker first appeared, he was managed by Brother Love. Later and more successfully, his manager was Paul Bearer (whose real name is William Moody, and who actually is a licensed embalmer and funeral director).

The Undertaker's entrances were spectacular. First, the lights would dim, and the funeral march would blare from the loudspeakers. Then the tubby, wild-eyed figure of Paul Bearer would appear, carrying an urn. Next, an oversized coffin was wheeled to ringside, and out of it would come the Undertaker himself.

He never hurried but would climb slowly into the ring and then intimidate and methodically demolish his opponent. The Undertaker was never an acrobatic or scientific wrestler with a variety of fast and flashy moves. At 6 feet 10 inches and 325 pounds, he is huge even in the professional wrestling world, and he uses his size and enormous strength to crush whoever stands in his way. His speciality was the casket match—the winner had to push his opponent into the coffin and slam the lid shut.

The Undertaker became a great favorite and actually won the WWF heavyweight championship twice, defeating Hulk Hogan in one of those bouts.

Early in his career, the Undertaker didn't talk much. He usually let Paul Bearer do the talking while he stood around and looked menacing. Occasionally he would come out with a one liner like "I will NOT rest in peace." He has become a bit more talkative recently, though not much more informative.

In response to a question about his past from writer Dan Murphy, he intoned gravely:

"Tell me, Mr. Murphy. Do you ever have nightmares?"

"I'm not sure I follow you."

"I have often heard writers characterized as troubled souls, sometimes living on the edge of madness. I assume you would consider yourself a writer . . . If you've had nightmares, you have glimpsed the soul of the Undertaker. I have a very special affinity for nightmares. . . ."

Spooky—but you don't learn much. And unlike Goldberg, the Undertaker never calls wrestling "fun." The Undertaker doesn't look like he would say anything was fun.

The story line, or mythology, surrounding the Undertaker is the most complex and confusing in the history of wrestling. After helping to make the Undertaker a major WWF star, Paul Bearer took up with a new discovery—Kane. Kane was about the same size and shape as the Undertaker, he had the same long hair and a similar outfit, though Kane's was red instead of black, and his face was obscured by a leather mask.

Paul Bearer said that Kane was the Undertaker's younger brother. He wore a mask because he had been horribly disfigured when he was a boy in a fire that had killed his parents and had been set by the Undertaker himself. The Undertaker believed that Kane had died in the blaze, but he had survived and returned in order to get revenge on the man who had ruined his life. Kane himself has never confirmed any of this because he doesn't speak at all. Paul Bearer later said that Kane was only the Undertaker's half brother, and that his father was manager Bearer himself.

That set off a series of well-publicized and very popular confrontations between Kane and the Undertaker, casket matches in which the loser was sealed in the casket and then set afire. It never quite got to that.

Somehow or other the gruesome pair was reconciled, and they began what has been described as a "reign of terror" over the WWF. That got the attention of "the Evil Owner," Vince McMahon, who recruited the pair for his war against Steve Austin, who had once been the Undertaker's tag team partner. (Are you still following this?) Together they defeated Austin, but they then refused to protect McMahon when he was beaten up by Austin. So the promoter forced the brothers to wrestle one another, and Austin was the referee. The Undertaker and Kane knocked one another out, and Austin declared himself the winner.

The Undertaker rehired Paul Bearer and confessed to setting the fire that had disfigured Kane, so the feud was on again. Kane appears to have gone over entirely to McMahon and become one of his most trusted and effective corporate bodyguards. The Undertaker is still gunning for McMahon, who he says cheated him out of a title belt.

Recently the Undertaker, led or at least assisted by Paul Bearer, seems to have formed a black robed doomsday cult, "the Ministry," which performs black-mass type ceremonies before matches and is able to control a crowd of other wrestlers called "the Acolytes" through some sort of evil power. The aim of the Ministry is to take over the WWF, and the Undertaker says that it is under the control of a power greater than himself.

Would the Undertaker care to explain what is going on?

"I've said enough now." He simply predicts that he will get his title back, and "the rest will rest in peace."

CHAPTER 10

Kane

Like so many wrestlers, the man who is now known as Kane has spent years searching for a successful persona. He was born Glen Jacobs in Knoxville, Tennessee. When he began his wrestling career in the late 1980s, it was as "Jim Powers." When he wrestled on a circuit in the mid South, it was as "Doomsday." In 1983 he made a onetime appearance in a WWF pay-per-view event as "the Black Knight." Then it was back to the minor leagues again as "Unabom." When he returned to the WWF, it was as "Isaac Yankem, the Evil Dentist," who had very bad teeth. It was a funny idea, but it didn't really catch on with the fans.

Then WWF management noticed that this

multinamed man bore a general resemblance to the enormously popular character the Undertaker. So he was given a new name and identity—Kane, the horribly mutilated brother (or half brother depending on what time you picked up the story line) of the Undertaker.

Kane is often billed as being a seven-foot giant—he's probably only about 6 feet 7 or 8 inches, but at 345 pounds he is huge, perhaps only an inch shorter than the Undertaker himself. Kane never speaks.

After a tangled, sometimes cooperative, sometimes violent relationship, Kane and the Undertaker have gone their separate ways. Kane has become the biggest and one of the most effective bodyguards of Mr. McMahon. The Undertaker and his occult group are trying to take control of the WWF from McMahon.

The saga of Kane and the Undertaker is sure to continue.

CHAPTER 11

"Macho Man" Randy Savage

Though he still appears in the ring occasionally, younger fans probably know Randy Savage, "the Macho Man," best from his commercial for a popular sausage snack. His appearance, muscles, huge sunglasses, funny hat, and wildly colored fringed jacket is fairly standard wrestling garb. But his voice is unmistakable—"Ohhhh, Yeahhhhh!!!"

"The Macho Man" was born Randy Poffo on November 15, 1952. He originally wanted to be a professional baseball player, and he spent five years in the St. Louis Cardinals, Cincinnati Reds, and Chicago White Sox minor league organizations before going into professional wrestling. This career choice is not a surprising one. His father,

Angelo Poffo, had been a tough professional wrestler. His brother, "Leapin'" Lanny Poffo, was a wrestling acrobat and wrestling poet laureate. (Leapin' Lanny would often recite some of his really bad verses before a match.)

The brothers kept their relationship a secret, more or less, and wrestled one another from time to time—usually with inconclusive results. Savage was, however, sometimes afflicted with his brother's poetry-writing urge. Here is an example: "I'll joust you with hustle and oust you with muscle; I'll tear you to shreds and leave you for dead: In this land I'm head honcho; Get on your knees to Macho."

Ouch!

Savage began his career in the South as a masked man called "The Spider." When he got to the WWF, his persona as "the Macho Man" had become firmly established. He was recognized as a fine wrestler, an absolutely superb interview subject, and a highly promotable individual. He was one of the most popular guests on Vince McMahon's wrestling talk show in the 1980s. Within a year, he was given a title match with Hulk Hogan. He didn't win, but that began a long rivalry between the two. "Macho Man" did eventually win the WWF championship, twice, but his reign as champ was not a long one either time.

Savage went over to the WCW at about the same time Hogan did, and the complex rivalry between them continued. "The Macho Man" has been in and out of the nWo. He won the WCW heavyweight championship but then was defeated by Hogan in April 1998.

Savage may have been the first professional wrestler to have a woman manager. (Gorgeous George had employed women valets to spray him with perfume and brush off his robe as he entered the ring.) In 1985 Randy Savage introduced the beautiful "Miss Elizabeth." In reality, Miss Elizabeth was Savage's wife, but that was a closely held secret within the wrestling world. Other women have since followed in her footsteps as wrestling managers.

There has always been some question as to whether Miss Elizabeth ever really did any managing. At first, she never said anything. She just stood around at ringside looking very attractive and very confused, even forlorn. "Macho Man" was always ordering her around, and on at least one occasion he flung her over his shoulder and carried her from the arena. Other wrestlers tried to protect her from Savage.

The competition over Miss Elizabeth became one of the persistent themes of Savage's career during the late 1980s. But Miss Elizabeth remained remarkably loyal, at least in the wrestling world. The two were actually divorced, though in public she remained at his side as manager. Recently, however, even this professional relationship seems to have broken up, and Miss Elizabeth is now being seen with the likes of Lex Luger and Scott Steiner. She's started talking too—and she has a beautiful voice.

CHAPTER 12

Ric Flair

Ric Flair has been a professional wrestler for over a quarter of a century. He was born in Minnesota on February 25, 1949, played football in college, and became a pro wrestler in 1972. He has won every available title, and many consider him the greatest wrestler of the modern era, perhaps the greatest wrestler ever.

He is at an age when most other wrestlers have long since hung up their boots and tights and gone into managing, promoting, or simply have retired from the wresting business completely. He doesn't need to prove anything to anyone, and he certainly doesn't need the money.

Flair has lost some of the speed and agility

that made him a champion, but he has never lost his fiercely competitive spirit. If pushed, and he has a short fuse, he is likely to strip off his beautifully tailored business suit and jump into the ring with someone half his age—and still win.

Flair's career is legendary. He used the nickname "the Nature Boy"—a tribute to the 1950s and '60s wrestler "Nature Boy" Buddy Rogers. Flair adopted Rogers's blond hair and arrogant strut as he entered the ring. Like Rogers, and Gorgeous George before him, the cocky man with the elaborately embroidered robe, Ric Flair became "the man you loved to hate."

Hate him or love him—he was good. Not only did he have all the moves, he had mastered the psychological side of wrestling. He looked like a winner, he acted like a winner, and his supreme confidence helped him win match after match.

His signature submission hold was the figure-four leglock. "Now we're going to school!" he would scream with a grin as he fixed the hold on his opponent's leg. Usually the match ended right there.

During the 1980s when the WWF came to dominate the wrestling scene on television, Flair was the NWA champ and that beleaguered organization's biggest star. He won his first NWA title on September 17, 1981, when he defeated the popular Dusty Rhodes. He lost the title several times to the likes of tough Harley Race and Kerry von Erich, but each time he fought back and finally regained the belt.

No one in the wrestling world had put his championship on the line more often or had a more grueling schedule than Ric Flair.

"He defends his title night after night, all over the globe," wrote wrestling expert George Napolitano. "In one week the champion has been known to put his title on the line in Charlotte, North Carolina, on Sunday afternoon; Toronto, Canada, on Sunday evening; and then depart for a tour of the Pacific to wrestle in New Zealand, Australia, Malaysia, and the Philippines."

Among Flair's many notable rivalries was one with Ricky Steamboat, another superb wrestler. Their final match ran a full sixty minutes and ended only when time ran out. When is the last time you saw a match with two wrestlers in the ring for an hour without outside interference or flashy gimmicks? Probably never. In the end, Flair retained his championship because there had been no decision.

Flair also formed one of the very first "outlaw groups" which have now become such a popular feature in wrestling. His group was "The Four Horsemen" with Arn Anderson, Ole Anderson, Tulle Blanchard and, of course, Ric Flair himself. The original group broke up in 1997, but the name "the Horsemen" has been adopted by other groups today.

In September 1991 the wrestling world was genuinely shocked when Flair, long the main prop of the NWA, finally decided that "if you can't beat 'em, join 'em" and skipped to Vince McMahon's WWF. But he was never really comfortable in the McMahon organization even though he captured the WWF championship twice, and in February 1993 he went over to the newly energized and financed WCW. In 1994 he was defeated for the WCW title by Hollywood (Hulk) Hogan.

These two wrestling icons have continued their rivalry, now as much out of the ring as in it. Hogan, of course, is the leader of his own outlaw group, the nWo. Flair has become the head of the entire WCW, or at least he has been the public face of the WCW recently. In one way or another, the pair has clashed again and again in offices, arena corridors, and empty fields. They are usually accompanied by their followers, henchmen, employees, or whatever, and this struggle has become a major theme of the WCW scenario.

For most of his career, the arrogant Flair was considered one of the bad guys, and Hogan the ultimate good guy. Now the roles have been reversed, and it is Flair who is the virtuous one, or at least as virtuous as any one gets in wrestling today, and at least for the moment.

CHAPTER 13

Mankind

Underneath the grotesque leather mask is Mickey Foley. Most wrestling fans don't know that name. He's also been known as Cactus Jack Manson, from Truth or Consequences, New Mexico, and Dude Love, a hippie ladies' man. He's had so many different identities that there are rumors that even he doesn't know who he really is anymore. Sometimes he has displayed two different personas in the same match, but wrestling fans immediately recognize the figure as Mankind (or ManKind, no one seems sure of how the name is supposed to be written), one of the most bizarre and unlikely figures in wrestling today.

Actually, the original Mickey Foley was

born on June 7, 1965, in Bloomington, Indiana, and raised on Long Island, New York. He graduated from the Cortland branch of New York State University and is married, with two children. Mankind, his wrestling persona, is a self-mutilating freak who lives in basements and talks to rats.

Mankind doesn't look much like a wrestler. Of course, lots of wrestlers wear masks, but not the kind of mask that Mankind wears; lots of wrestlers have long scraggly hair, but not quite as scraggly as Mankind's; and lots of wrestlers have gimmicks—but a sock puppet called Mr. Socko? His costume is—well, tacky is about the best thing you can say about it: a tattered, short-sleeved white shirt, out of date tie, and Goodwill-style pants and boots. He is the fashion opposite of one of his chief foes, The Rock.

Mankind doesn't look like much of a wrestler in his funny clothes, especially when compared to the stripped down, heavily muscled bodybuilder types or the 400-pound behemoths. He's a big guy, 6 feet 2 inches and nearly 280 pounds, but as Mankind he doesn't look that big. He can look small, shambling, and almost pathetic when compared to some of his opponents. Appearance is deceiving, for Mankind is a strong, skillful, and at times extremely acrobatic wrestler.

Mickey Foley's idol, when he was growing up, was the great Superfly Jimmy Snuka whose trademark was high-flying acrobatic leaps off the ring ropes. He once even hitchhiked hundreds of miles to see the Superfly live, and he spent a lot of time trying to imitate the Superfly's moves. Though he has never really matched his idol's famous leaps, he has used them to great advantage.

But most of all, Mankind is known for his ability to absorb tremendous punishment and come back fighting, again and again. Like that pink bunny in the battery commercials, he just keeps on going.

As Cactus Jack he had some exceptionally brutal matches with a huge man known as Vader. In one bout in Germany he got his head caught between the ropes and lost part of his left ear. As Mankind he received a broken jaw and lost three teeth in a 1988 cage match with the Undertaker. He is a living, breathing, and sometimes bleeding testament to the fact that wrestling is not all "fake."

In 1995 and 1996 this wrestler did a memorable stint with Extreme Championship Wrestling (ECW), one of the more violent organizations. When he came to the WWF, he excelled in hardcore matches, which have even fewer rules than other matches, and was, for a time, WWF Hardcore Champion.

One of the most bizarre elements of this most bizarre wrestler's matches is his use of a childhood toy, the sock puppet he called "Mr. Socko." At a critical moment in a match, Mankind will pull Mr. Socko out of his pants, slip it on his hand, and then try to force that hand down an opponent's throat. Officially, the hold is called "the Mandible Claw" and it's usually a finishing move for Mankind.

Mankind was swept into and then out of Vince McMahon's favor. For a while, he was Mr. McMahon's most loyal corporate follower. He wasn't doing it only for the money, as most of McMahon's other followers freely admit they are. He seemed to love McMahon and regarded him as sort of a surrogate father. He visited McMahon in the hospital after the boss had injured his leg in a run in with Steve Austin, and even bought him a

Father's Day gift, a leaf blower. It's hard to imagine the Evil Owner of the WWF out there cleaning up his driveway on weekends, but Mankind seemed to think it was appropriate. By the time Mankind had the gift, he had been double crossed by McMahon when the boss and his corporation rigged matches to favor their new recruit, the Rock. McMahon even stole Mr. Socko, who somehow wound up as a headband for another strange wrestling toy, Al Snow's "The Head"—a dummy head which Snow uses to clobber opponents.

But as the scenario unfolded, it turned out that McMahon had underestimated the strange figure of Mankind. The wrestler absorbed all the punishment that McMahon's Team Corporate was able to dish out, and he came back for more. Mankind even went on to win the WWF Heavyweight title, although he held it only briefly.

In professional wrestling today, a wrestler's ultimate success depends upon the degree to which he can engage and excite the fans. If they fill the seats in the auditorium or watch his matches on TV and boost the wrestling show's ratings, he's going to move up. The strangest twist of all in Mankind's career is that this odd-looking figure in the leather mask and ratty white shirt has become a real fan favorite. People love him just because he seems so crazy. That's why he is likely to remain at the top of the heap for some time to come.

CHAPTER 14

The Rock

Professional wrestlers always seem to be forgetting the past (and hoping the fans forget it as well) and reinventing themselves as entirely new characters. In reality, however, professional wrestlers cherish tradition, and there are a large number of second or third generation wrestlers. Such a figure is Rocky Maivia, now better known as "The Rock," one of the fastest rising stars in the WWF.

Rocky Maivia was born in Florida, the son of Rocky "Soulman" Johnson, who had wrestled very successfully all over the United States during the 1970s and early 80s. At one point during his career, Rocky Johnson joined up as tag-team partner with one of the great Samoan wrestlers, High Chief Peter

Maivia. The pair drew huge crowds on the West Coast, in Phoenix, and in Las Vegas.

Johnson married Maivia's daughter, and they had a son. The couple later split, and the boy adopted his mother's name, Maivia. Young Rocky developed as an outstanding athlete and seemed destined for a career in the NFL; a back injury prevented that, but he did play pro ball in Canada. Then tradition took over, and he entered the world of professional wrestling.

When Rocky Maivia first became a wrestler, he was about as nice a guy as you could meet. He gave long polite interviews, signed autographs for fans, and smiled and waved a lot. He also wrestled extremely well. But in today's wrestling world, nice guys don't get noticed, even if they are great wrestlers. So rather abruptly, nice guy Rocky Maivia was transformed into "The Rock," one of the most unpleasant and egotistical figures in the wrestling world—and since wrestling is filled with unpleasant egotists, that is really saying something.

"The Rock"—he always refers to himself in the third person, as if he were some distant and godlike figure—has demonstrated a remarkable talent for antagonizing others. And he's certainly getting noticed. Right now, he is probably the hottest young wrestler in the WWF, and he is certainly the most successful.

"Just take a look at me," he says. "I'm handsome, well built, in better physical shape than many wrestlers. I have everything going for me, and that's why they call me 'the Rock.' I am solid muscle. I am practically undefeated, and the majority of the wrestling world is insanely jealous of me. Don't deny it." Bragging, sure, but also very close to the truth.

His signature statement, "Do you smell what the Rock's got cooking?" has become one of the most popular catchphrases in wrestling today.

But most of all, it's the eyebrow. The Rock has one amazingly active eyebrow. He stares out at the crowd or the camera and lifts his right eyebrow halfway to his hairline. The result is an expression that mixes arrogance and amazement. It says, "I am the greatest wrestler the world has ever known, and I can't understand why everyone in the world doesn't recognize this." This feat has been called "the People's Eyebrow" and later "the Corporate Eyebrow." But it's basically "the Rock's Eyebrow."

The Rock stands in the ring while people

in the auditorium are jeering him and throwing things, and he talks about his thousands of fans in the auditorium and millions watching on television.

And he's not far wrong. Despite those who deride him as "The Crock," Rocky Maivia is picking up a real following. He even did a guest shot on the Fox sitcom *That Seventies Show*. TV crossovers are a sign that a wrestler has really arrived.

The Rock, no longer Mr. Nice Guy, had appeared for a while as part of The Nation of Domination, but he was destined to go solo and on to bigger things.

After the Nation dissolved, the Rock proclaimed himself "People's Champion," but then the Rock became involved in the complex and long-running saga of Vince McMahon's attempts to humiliate Steve Austin. The Rock became one of Mr. McMahon's Team Corporate. He's unapologetic about his new role. "Look, business is business, and I know who signs my fat paychecks. And he's smart to have me because he knows I'm one of the best. McMahon and his associates didn't just choose me out of the blue. They know I agree with their thinking, and that I have the strength, power, and ability to get things done."

McMahon has done a lot for the Rock as well. He has arranged matches in a way that favors wins by the Rock, and other members of the Corporation have stepped in to help the Rock gain the WWF championship belt.

The Rock has gone from People's Champion to Corporate Champion. But The Rock's Corporate associations do not mean that he can't wrestle, or that he isn't one of the most exciting and entertaining personalities in wrestling today.

His series of early 1999 matches with Mankind were absolute classics, if not of scientific wrestling, then of mayhem and surprise. They were sports entertainment at its absolute best.

Anyone who follows wrestling knows that it is utterly foolish to predict what's going to happen next. That's why so many people love wrestling. By the time you read this, the Rock may be Mr. McMahon's chief nemesis. But one thing is safe to predict: Barring serious injury, the Rock is going to be one of the top professional wrestlers in the world at the dawn of the new Millennium.

CHAPTER 15

Bam Bam Bigelow

He's just your average 380-pound guy with a shaved head that is elaborately tattooed with flames. That's Bam Bam Bigelow, one of the toughest men in wrestling.

Before taking up wrestling, Scott Bigelow was a professional bounty hunter; he hunted down human fugitives for a price. Wrestling columnist Dave Rosenbaum commented recently, "Wrestling isn't safer than too many professions, but it is safer than being a bounty hunter, especially a bounty hunter in Mexico."

From the start, Bigelow was a hard-nosed brawler, known as the "Beast from the East." He would do anything to win a match, and sometimes he would do anything to lose one.

A lot of wrestlers get very coy or even angry when they are accused of taking part in a "fixed" match. Not Bam Bam. In 1995 he was a headliner at the WWF pay-per-view WrestleMania XI. His opponent was the great New York Giants linebacker Lawrence Taylor.

Taylor was a big, strong man, but he had never wrestled before, and he should not have been able to stay in the ring for five minutes with an even bigger and more experienced brawler like Bam Bam. Still, Bam Bam lost, and the fans were all over him. Bam Bam's reply was, "You should see the check I got!" It was his biggest payday ever. The match was a throwback to the old carnival days when the pro would be paid to take a dive in a match with the local favorite.

Bigelow moved over to the ECW where he compiled an impressive record against some of the really tough guys in that organization. His favorite move was throwing his bloodied opponent out of the ring and into the audience. He has a real core of fans among the more devoted or obsessed of the hardcore wrestling fanatics. However, the ECW is not a major TV operation, and it's hard for a wrestler to develop a national following if he isn't on TV regularly with either the WCW or WWF. So late in 1998, Bigelow was back in the big time again—but only as a member of the audience.

Bam Bam began showing up in the audience at Goldberg's matches, screaming threats and challenges at the reigning WCW champ. He would even try to rush the ring. At one point, he trashed Goldberg's dressing room and later attacked him in the parking lot, but he was never able to beat Goldberg in the ring.

Bam Bam Bigelow is like a blast from the past of the old days of 'rasslin. He moves from organization to organization, city to city, never staying in one place very long. He's not interested in selling T-shirts or action figures. He creates havoc wherever he goes but rarely sticks around long enough to win a championship or pick up a regular following. He just collects his paycheck and moves on.

CHAPTER 16

Goldust

Okay, let's try to sort this out for the uninitiated. The man who was to become Goldust (or Golddust) is named Dustin Runnels, the son of the extraordinarily popular Dusty "The American Dream" Rhodes, who was a wrestling star a generation ago. Since tradition counts a great deal in wrestling, and since the boy (born on April 11, 1966, in Austin, Texas) grew up to stand 6-feet 6-inches tall and weigh over 250 pounds, it was practically inevitable that he would go into wrestling just like his father.

He began his wrestling career in Florida in 1988 as "The Natural." Later, he became a tag-team partner of Ricky "The Dragon"

Steamboat, forming an extremely successful partnership, and the pair briefly held the world tag-team title. When Runnels subsequently teamed up with Barry Windham, the partnership was equally successful.

Then, in October 1995, things began getting really strange for Dustin Runnels. He began appearing in the WWF as "Goldust," wearing a gold lamé costume, a long blond wig, outrageous makeup, and he was accompanied by his manager, Marlena, a tough, sexy, cigar-smoking woman—who also happened to be his real wife, Alexandra York.

Goldust quickly became one of the most recognizable figures in the WWF. (With that outfit he was certainly not going to go unnoticed!) He was jeered, reviled, even spat upon—all of which meant that he excited the fans, and in wrestling that's the name of the game. Goldust even won a minor championship.

Then, in 1998, Goldust disappeared and was replaced by Dustin Runnels. In this incarnation, Runnels "got religion." He was a God-fearing, born-again Christian continually preaching against many of the things that were going on in the wrestling world. He wore jeans, a T-shirt, and looked remarkably like his famous father. He was now accompanied by his wife, Terri Runnels, the former Marlena and former Alexandra York.

In wrestling today, virtue is rarely rewarded. The virtuous Runnels was not a successful wrestler, never became a fan favorite, and his wife ran off with swivel-hipped Val Venus. By late 1998 Runnels was gone and Goldust was back—with a vengeance. He was meaner, nastier, more independent, and more successful than ever. He was determined to get Val Venus, and the pair had several notable bouts. At one point, Goldust took off his long blond wig and threw it at Venus. Under the wig was closely cropped blond hair, and Goldust now regularly appears without the wig—though he looks nearly as weird as before.

Goldust came back, and so did Marlena. The cigar-smoking beauty showed up, unannounced, at a match with Steve Regal and began cheering her estranged husband.

The reincarnated Goldust is more popular than ever and certainly more popular than the hapless Dustin Runnels.

What's next for this strange figure in the gold suit?

"Goldust will do what he has to do to be successful," he told *The Wrestler* magazine. "You should never be too certain what Goldust may do next."

CHAPTER 17

Sting

"Real Men Wear Facepaint"

That's the motto on one of Sting's many fan Web sites. This enigmatic wrestler (real name Steve Borden), who enjoys extraordinary fan popularity, made his professional debut in 1985. At first, he was only a regional favorite but on March 27, 1988, Sting wrestled the legendary Ric Flair to a 45-minute draw on a nationally televised pay-per-view event. It made him a superstar.

Sting, at 6 feet 3 inches and 260 pounds approachs his matches and the interviews which form such a big part of any wrestler's popularity with tremendous enthusiasm. His facepaint changes regularly. His in-the-ring tactics, featuring the "Stinger splash" and "scorpion leglock," bring fans to their feet and opponents to their knees. Sting's name was not drawn from the name of the popular rock star of the time but from the scorpion, the insect with a deadly sting in its tail. In the ring he could be deadly.

Sting became as popular in the NWA and WCW as Hulk Hogan was in the WWF. He won two world titles and attracted millions of fans. His legion of "little Stingers" was almost as large as Hogan's legion of "Hulka-maniacs." Sales of Sting T-shirts, masks, and other name paraphernalia went through the roof.

Unlike stars such as Hogan and Flair, Sting did not appear constantly and keep himself in the public eye. By the mid 1990s, he began a series of extended and mysterious disap-pearances, and his reappearances were just as mysterious. He would suddenly show up in a cloud of smoke or be lowered from the ceil-ing of the auditorium. He became a new, darker, and more enigmatic figure. His face-paint featured the red and black colors of the nWo Wolfpack, and he began a complex and hard-to-fathom relationship with them, a group containing many of his old enemies.

Recently, Sting has disappeared from the

wrestling scene completely. His fans insist that since Steve Borden is a family man, he has other responsibilities to take care of. But they promise that the man of mystery will be back—soon.

Perhaps he already is.

CHAPTER 18
Scott Steiner

Scott Steiner is one of those guys who looks like his muscles have muscles. He claims to have the biggest arms in the world, and he may be right. Steiner loves those muscles! He flexes his arm and kisses his bulging biceps, and that may be the purest expression of true love that you will ever find in the wrestling world. Steiner has so many muscles that he doesn't just look strong—he looks strange. When he's in the ring, people hold up signs which read "GENETIC FREAK."

If there is anything bigger than Scott Steiner's muscles, it's his ego. Even in a world of monumental egos, Steiner manages to stand out. The Fabulous Moolah, the greatest woman wrestler in history says, "Scott Steiner's muscles are sure nice to look at, darlin' and doesn't he know it. I mean, his head is so big that he has to step out of the room to change his mind."

Scott Steiner has been around wrestling for years, most of that time as part of the tag team the Steiner Brothers. Scott and his brother, Rick (they really are brothers, and their family name was originally Rechsteiner) came out of the University of Michigan's wrestling program, and they formed what was arguably the finest tag team in wrestling history. They were champions in the old NWA, the WWF, and more recently in the WCW.

The Steiners were fast, athletic, and most of all they had the smooth working relationship necessary to be successful in tag-team matches. But in wrestling few relationships last forever, and the Steiner team lasted longer than most. Eventually, Scott Steiner, always the bigger and more dominant of the pair, turned on his brother and double-crossed him, either because he craved more individual acclaim, or because the lords of wrestling determined that the public had become bored with the Steiner team and decided to shake things up by adding a little more excitement and confusion to the Steiner saga.

Scott Steiner, now a fixture of the outlaw nWo, began calling himself "Big Poppa Pump." He even had the title emblazoned on the back of his trunks. Rick became the "Dogfaced Gremlin" and took to wearing a large dog collar.

During 1998 the Steiner saga took any number of strange and unexpected turns, but nothing as strange and unexpected as the Bagwell connection. Scott Steiner teamed up with Buff Bagwell, a sometime wrestling partner and full-time promoter and court jester for Big Poppa Pump. Rick showed up with another Bagwell as his prospective wrestling partner—Judy Bagwell, Buff's mother. She was a feisty middle aged lady who had apparently never wrestled anything more dangerous than a grocery bag in her life. Mrs. Bagwell somehow wound up in the hospital before any brother-to-brother, mother-to-son match ever took place.

As 1999 dawned, Scott Steiner was having his problems. His brother had defeated him, and Goldberg had taken up his challenge and demolished Big Poppa Pump. Goldberg had some outside help from Scott's brother,

Rick, but he clearly and decisively dominated Scott from the start of the match.

Will the Steiner brothers ever get back together again as a team? Don't bet on it. But then don't bet against it. It is the sheer wild, improbable, and unpredictable nature of the wrestling scene that makes it so much fun.

CHAPTER 19
Diamond Dallas Page

Diamond Dallas Page, or DDP, was originally a wrestling manager. Actually, he was originally Page Falkenberg of Tampa, Florida. At 6 feet 5 inches and well over 250 pounds, he looks like someone who would naturally become a wrestler. But he began his wrestling career in the 1980s with the old AWA as manager for the popular team of the Freebirds. Later, when Scott Hall was wrestling under the name "The Diamond Studd" in 1990, Dallas Page was his manager; then Hall became "Razor Ramon" and went over to the WCW. It wasn't until 1991 that the onetime manager who had no one left to manage entered the ring himself, a reversal of the usual career path where former wrestlers become managers.

Page started in the WCW as part of a team called "The Vegas Connection." His partner was another really big man, Vinnie Vegas, later "Diesel," and now known as Kevin Nash.

Wrestling is in DDP's family now. His wife, Kimberly Falkenberg, was once known as "The Booty Babe," valet to "The Booty Man," and as "The Diamond Doll," valet to Jonnie B. Badd. She has since become one of the Nitro girls, a top WCW attraction.

DDP has had a very successful career, and his finishing maneuver, "the diamond cutter," is one of the most feared in wrestling.

Unlike his two former associates Hall and Nash, DDP has never become part of the nWo or any other outlaw faction. As a result, he has frequently been attacked by members of outlaw groups.

In 1998 Page got a chance to wrestle another old friend, Goldberg, for the WCW heavyweight championship. He wasn't able to beat the champ, who was wrestling at the top of his form, but the match was a classic, certainly one of the best of the year. And it wasn't settled with a gimmick.

There is even a rumor that DDP has been doing some charity work. But in today's wrestling world a rumor like that could ruin a guy's reputation.

CHAPTER 20

Scott Hall

In his career, which began in 1986, Scott Hall has been "Starship Coyote" and "The Diamond Studd." He even held the AWA world tag-team championship for several months. But he didn't really achieve major success until he became someone else.

In May 1992 he switched to the WWF as "Razor Ramon," a swaggering "Cuban" wrestler who would usually enter the ring chewing a toothpick that he would contemptuously throw into his opponent's face. His finishing move was called "The Razor's Edge." This was a gimmick that caught on with the fans, and Hall began to get the attention that had eluded him for so long.

The real Scott Hall was born in Miami,

Florida, on October 20, 1959. He's one of
wrestling's big men at 6 feet 7 inches and
287 pounds. (It comes as no surprise that he
was a basketball player in college.)

As Razor Ramon, Hall dominated the
Intercontinental Championship, defeating
such stalwarts as Rick Martel, Jeff Jarett, and
Diesel, aka Kevin Nash. He had a notable
match with Shawn Michaels in WrestleMania XI, a ladder match that he won with
relative ease, but it ended when he took a
spectacular fall from the top of the ladder
into the ring.

In 1996, now using his own name, Scott
Hall went over to the WCW and became one
of the founders of the "outlaw" nWo. He
may not be Razor Ramon anymore, but Big
Scott Hall can still swagger with the best of
them.

CHAPTER 21

Kevin Nash

Kevin Nash likes to be called "Big Sexy." At 7 feet 1 inch and 367 pounds, he is certainly big. Sexy is a matter of personal taste.

He was born on July 9, 1960, in Las Vegas, Nevada, though he was raised in the colder climate of Southgate, Michigan. He played basketball for the University of Tennessee and worked as a nightclub bouncer.

He began his wrestling career with the WCW, and at first it didn't go too well. He started as "Steel," half of a tag team called "The Master Blasters." The other half was "Blade." Then he was "Oz" in a mask and green cape, and after that he was Vinnie Vegas, an oversized Las Vegas lounge lizard.

Few remember these early incarnations of the big man.

Things went better when he switched to the WWF in 1993 and began appearing as "Diesel," bodyguard for the popular Shawn Michaels, and as Diesel he briefly held the WWF championship.

When he went back to Ted Turner's WCW, he was Kevin Nash again; he became ally of his old foe Hollywood (Hulk) Hogan, and he was a founding member of the nWo. At last report, he was still with the nWo, and he became the man to end Goldberg's unbeaten streak, though he needed a lot of help from his friends. He briefly held the nWo heavyweight championship before quite literally turning it over to Hogan.

CHAPTER 22

Saturn

It would not surprise any wrestling fan to know that Perry Saturn grew up in the housing projects in a tough part of Cleveland and was often in trouble with the law when he was young. Fans would be more surprised to learn that he has a bachelor's degree in criminology from Ohio State University and at one time aspired to be a police officer, a tribute to the cop who had helped him when he was a street kid. Actually, most of today's big-time wrestlers have college degrees, though they don't talk about that a lot. Being a college man hurts the tough guy image.

Saturn doesn't have to worry. He is an authentic tough guy. According to the official WCW magazine, by the time he was 17

Perry Saturn had already spent five years in detention homes. At that point he faced a choice: He could either spend another year in a home or four years in the Army. A Cleveland cop named Ron Turner, who had befriended Saturn and taught him martial arts, told him to take the Army. Saturn enrolled in one of the most demanding training programs, Ranger Training and Airborne School, and he got through it.

After the Army, Saturn worked at some dead-end manual labor jobs, and his thoughts turned to his boyhood ambition of becoming a professional wrestler. He applied to a training center run by wrestling legend Killer Kowalski, but Kowalski told the young man that at 165 pounds he was too small to become a professional wrestler. Saturn refused to give up—he wanted to prove Kowalski wrong.

He put on 20 pounds and moved to Boston just to be near Kowalski's gym. He paid Kowalski his entire fee up front, spent the next year training, and because he was broke, he slept in his car.

Still, it wasn't easy for a man Saturn's size to make a successful career in pro wrestling. But now, in his early thirties, and weighing a muscular 230 pounds he is considered a genuine rising star in the WCW.

"I feel I am one of the hardest-training wrestlers around. I practice kempo karate, judo, and watch hundreds of videotapes. I'm constantly trying to learn. When I'm done wrestling, I want to know everything there is to know about it; that's my goal."

In the meantime, an awful lot of other wrestlers are discovering how much Perry Saturn has already learned.

CHAPTER 23

Chris Jericho

What is it that makes Chris Jericho so repulsive? He's a good wrestler, strong, fast, agile, and utterly fearless. He's small for a big-time wrestler—cruiserweight class: 6 feet 2 inches, about 225 pounds. Even so, he's ready to climb into the ring with men much larger than he is, often getting severely beaten in the process. His nickname, "Lion Heart," is not just bravado.

Sure, he's got an ego, insisting that every fan in the world is a "Jerichoholic" when actually they despise him. He'll use any tactic or trick to win a match, and do everything he can not only to beat but to humiliate an opponent and bad mouth him afterwards.

Jericho certainly carries a grudge, but in wrestling today that's the way practically everyone acts.

So why do people hate him?

Maybe it's his hair, which looks like his hair stylist certainly hates him. But wrestling fans have seen much worse.

Maybe its Ralphus, Jericho's bodyguard, or companion, or something. But Ralphus doesn't really do anything except stand around looking like one of those relatives your family doesn't want to talk about.

And maybe it's all of the above and more. Chris Jericho is brash, arrogant, obnoxious, spiteful, and wears a permanent sneer. Jericho seems to have a God-given talent for getting under people's skins. You may hate him, but you have to notice him. In wrestling, the competitor who inspires strong emotions in the fans, be they love or hate, is going to be noticed and will rise quickly in his chosen profession. That's why Jericho is one of the fastest rising young wrestlers operating today. In his relatively short career, Jericho has won and lost more titles than most wrestlers get a shot at in an entire lifetime.

Though Jericho was born on Long Island, he was raised in Canada. His father, Ted Irvine, was a National Hockey League player with teams in Boston, Los Angeles, St. Louis, and New York. As an ardent fan in his youth, Jericho always wanted to become a wrestler, but he met Jesse Ventura, who advised him to get some other kind of training first, just in case pro wrestling didn't work out. So he got a journalism degree—then he became a wrestler.

He began his pro career in 1990 in Canada and then wrestled extensively in Mexico, where the lighter-weight wrestlers are more popular, as well as in Japan and Germany. He wrestled in lodge halls and unheated arenas while suffering from serious injuries received in the ring. In short, he paid his dues.

Jericho made his debut with the ECW in February 1996, and he went on to wrestle the top men in that organization, including many of the big guys like Bam Bam Bigelow. By August, he was wrestling in the WCW against the likes of Eddy Guerrero, Dean Malenko, Ray Misterio, Jr., Booker T, and even the huge Diamond Dallas Page. He didn't defeat all of them, but every opponent who has faced Chris Jericho knows that he has been in a fight.

Chris Jericho may be unlovable, but he is one tough guy, and for that he deserves respect. Wrestling isn't a warm and fuzzy occupation.

About the Author

Daniel Cohen is the author of more than 160 books for both young readers and adults, and he is the former managing editor of *Science Digest* magazine. His titles include *Ghostly Tales of Love and Revenge; Ghosts of the Deep; The Ghost of Elvis and Other Celebrity Spirits; The Ghosts of War; Phantom Animals; Phone Call from a Ghost: Strange Tales from Modern America,* and *Real Ghosts,* all available from Minstrel Books, *Hollywood Dinosaur* and *The Millennium,* available from Archway Paperbacks.

Mr. Cohen was born in Chicago and has a degree in journalism from the University of Illinios. He has lectured at colleges and universities throughout the country. Mr. Cohen lives with his wife in New Jersey.

IT'S HUGE. IT'S GLOBAL. IT'S...

THE MILLENNIUM

By
Daniel Cohen

When it comes to the subject everyone is talking about, this book tells *all*!

Which cities will host the biggest millennial blasts?

Will the Millennium virus make all of the world's computers crash?

What is the Doomsday Prophecy? And what happened on New Year's Eve in the year 999? It's not what you think!

It's not just another New Year's Eve. It's the year 2000. Where will *you* be when the clock strikes midnight?

From Archway Paperbacks
Published by Pocket Books